THE HEMPLEMAGIC

COACH STEVE

Copyright © 2025

Coach Steve

eBook ISBN: 978-1-967106-00-4
Paperback ISBN: 978-1-967106-01-1
Hardcover ISBN: 978-1-967106-02-8

All Rights Reserved. Any unauthorized reprint or use of this material is strictly prohibited. No part of this book may be reproduced or transmitted in any form or by any means, electronic or mechanical, including photocopying, recording, or by any information storage and retrieval system without express written permission from the author.

All reasonable attempts have been made to verify the accuracy of the information provided in this publication. Nevertheless, the author assumes no responsibility for any errors and/or omissions.

The story began many years ago in a town called Data, located in Nebraska, U.S.A. Data appeared to be a normal place, with tree-lined streets, houses, and buildings. All the people were so nice and warm. Over on Post Road lived an old woman named Gertrude—though she preferred to be called GG. Across the road lived the 7-year-old twins, Jack and Avery. Dogs played in the puddles, and the town of Data was just waking up. You could smell the freshly cut grass and hear the milk truck passing by.

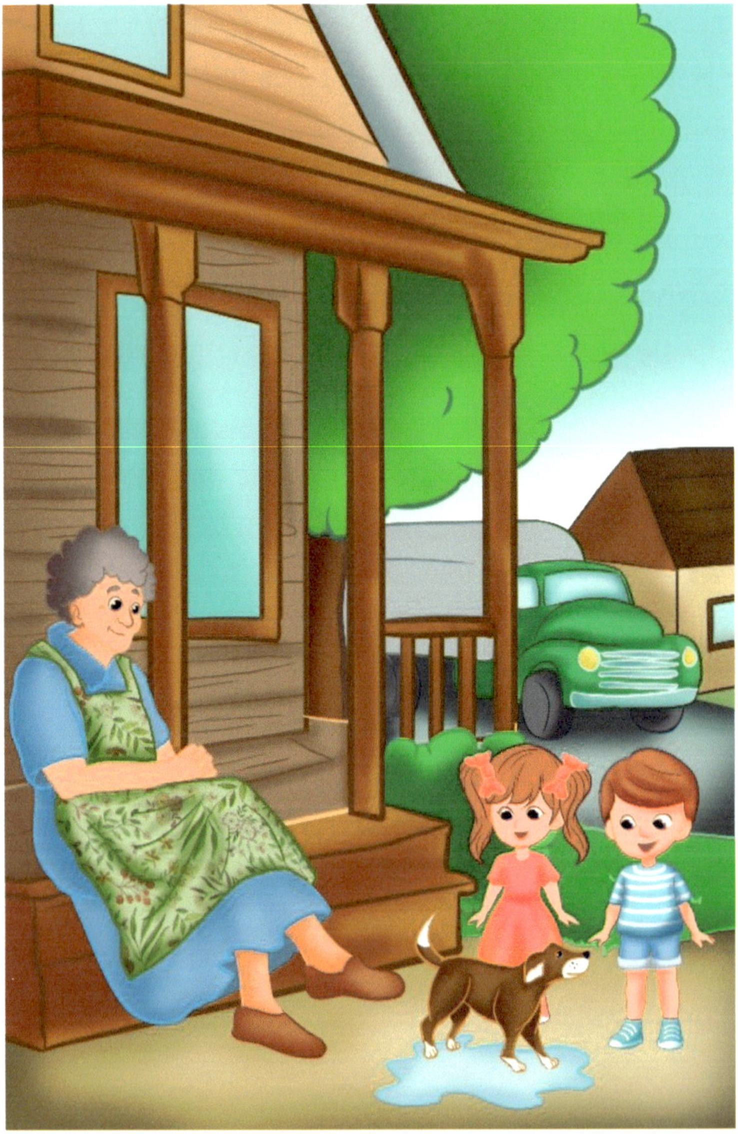

But today would not be a normal day in Data.

Big Pops was the mayor of Data, and he was always happy, spreading joy wherever he went. However, today, when Big Pops came to town, he wasn't smiling and seemed very worried. As Big Pops walked through the town, everyone noticed that he wasn't smiling or waving. He looked concerned.

When Big Pops strolled past old lady GG, she called out, as always, "Hi, Big Pops!" She waited for her usual response, but today, there was no "Good morning" in return. Miss GG thought to herself, *Big Pops isn't very happy today.*

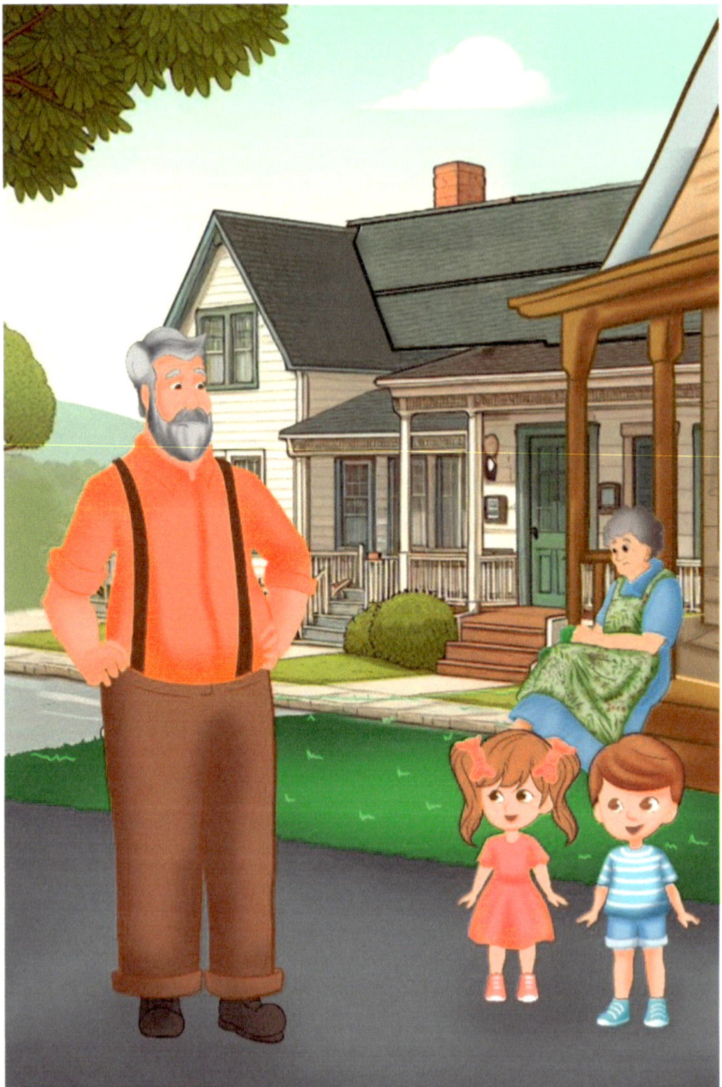

Big Pops kept walking and passed the twins, Bill and Eedee. They ran up to him with their big, bright smiles, shouting excitedly about their new baby brother, Stevie. But today, they were confused—Big Pops didn't even notice them.

Finally, Big Pops arrived at his destination, far outside town at the end of Hudson Logan Forest. He entered the forest and walked deep inside, heading toward the tallest tree—the biggest tree in the forest. It was so tall that it reached the fluffy white clouds.

Big Pops took out his binoculars, which he jokingly called his "silly glasses" because they made faraway things look close. He looked up at the giant tree, and way up on a branch, nestled in the clouds, he saw a nest with three eggs.

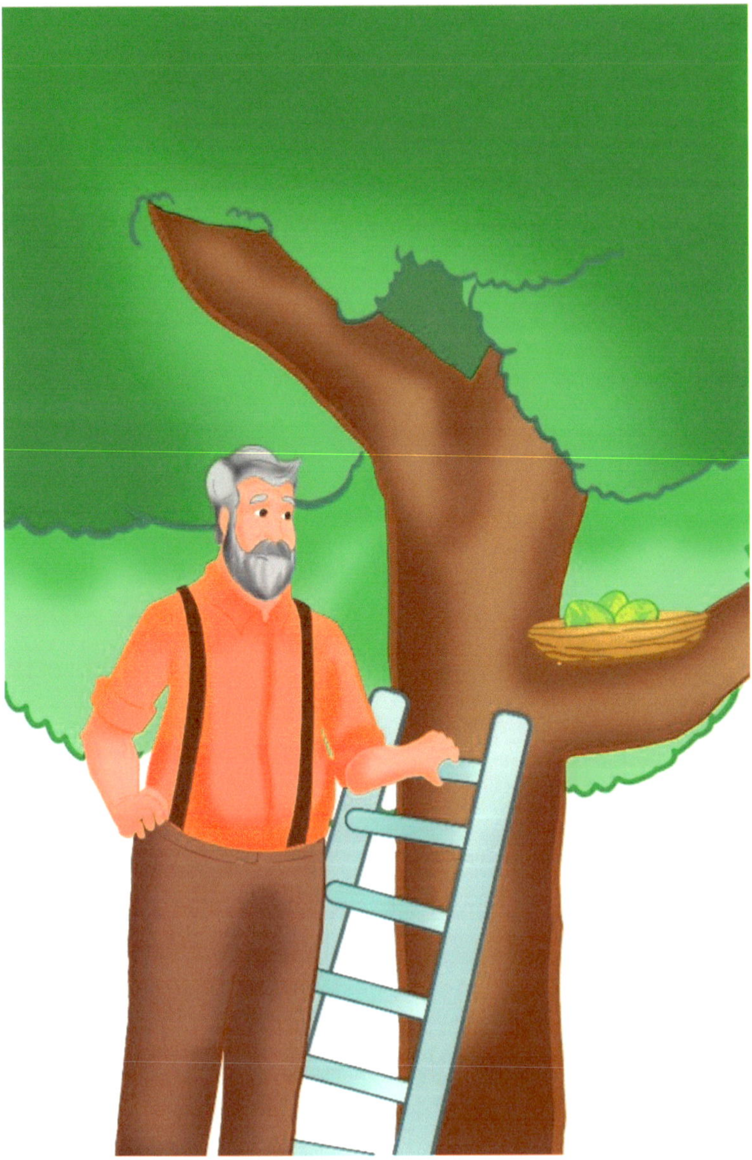

Big Pops leaned a very tall ladder against the tree and climbed higher and higher until he reached the nest. He carefully placed the eggs in a special bag, then climbed back down the tall ladder, holding the bag of eggs with great care.

He quickly headed back toward town. Just as he reached the old bridge on the outskirts, a familiar car pulled up behind him. One glance and Big Pops knew it was Mama Grams. She drove a large, colorless car, and everyone called her Grammy. Grammy rolled down her window and cheerfully offered Big Pops a ride. At first, he declined, but Grammy was hard to say no to.

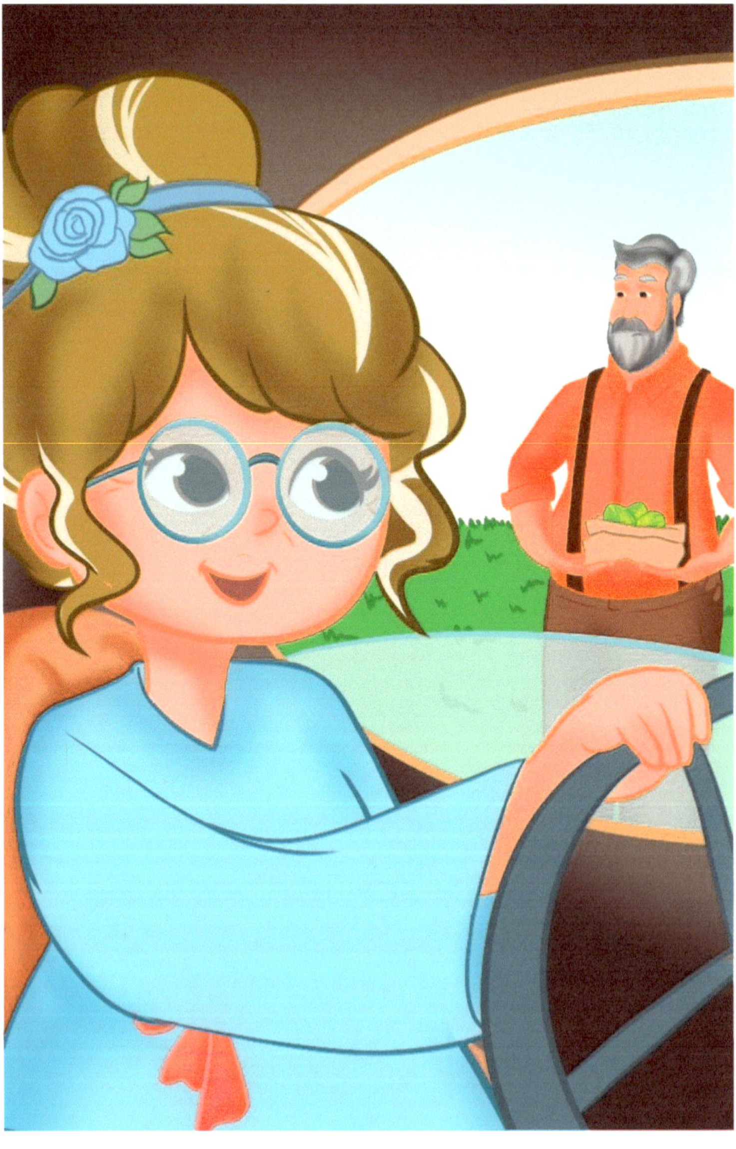

Big Pops finally agreed to ride with her, but only if she would take him straight to Doc Brian's with no stops. "Please, don't stop for anyone," Big Pops insisted.

Grammy, curious, asked, "Why would you need the town veterinarian?"

Big Pops hesitated but eventually said he'd rather not answer. Grammy, stubborn and curious as a cat, refused to move the car until he told her. Nervously, Big Pops showed her the special eggs.

They arrived at Doc Brian's office, where animals were everywhere, as usual. Two billy goats were being mischievous, and ducks wandered about. Four dogs—Bentley, Marley, Xena, and Jeeter—were there too.

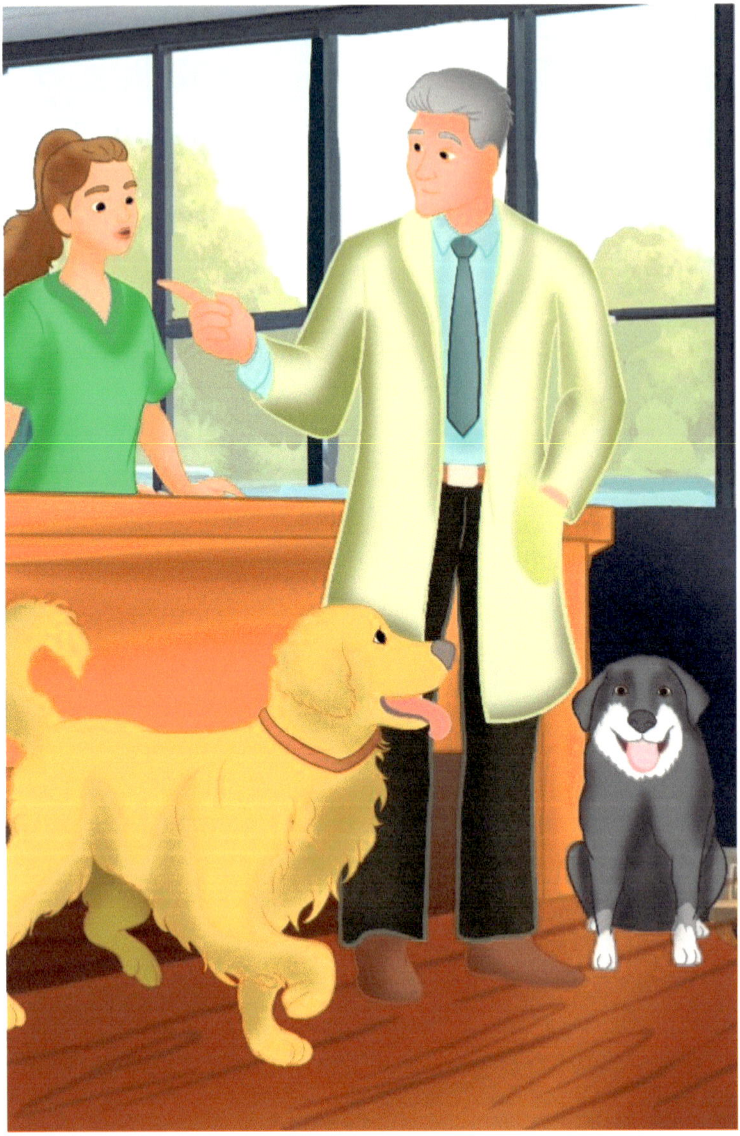

Pops and Grammy walked into the office, holding the special bag with the three large green eggs wrapped in a blanket. As always, behind the desk was Nurse Megan, who was busy scolding Marley for chasing the ducks.

Marley was one of the four dogs Doc Brian owned. The other three were Bentley, Jeeter, and Xena. Xena usually followed Marley's lead in everything he did. Bentley, being older, didn't chase the animals; he just watched over them, almost as if he smiled whenever Marley, Xena, or Jeeter got scolded.

Nurse Megan was so busy she didn't even notice Pops, Grammy, or the special bag with the three green eggs. Pops and Grammy just walked into a room and waited for Doc Brian.

While they waited, Harvey, the resident billy goat, came for a visit, followed as always by Edna, the chicken.

Finally, Doc Brian came into the room, chased out Harvey and Edna, and shut the door.

Pops waited for Grammy to put a blanket on the special table that Doc Brian used to examine animals. Then Pops softly placed the eggs on the blanket, one by one. Doc Brian's eyes got wider and wider as Pops put the first, then the second, and finally the third egg on the blanket.

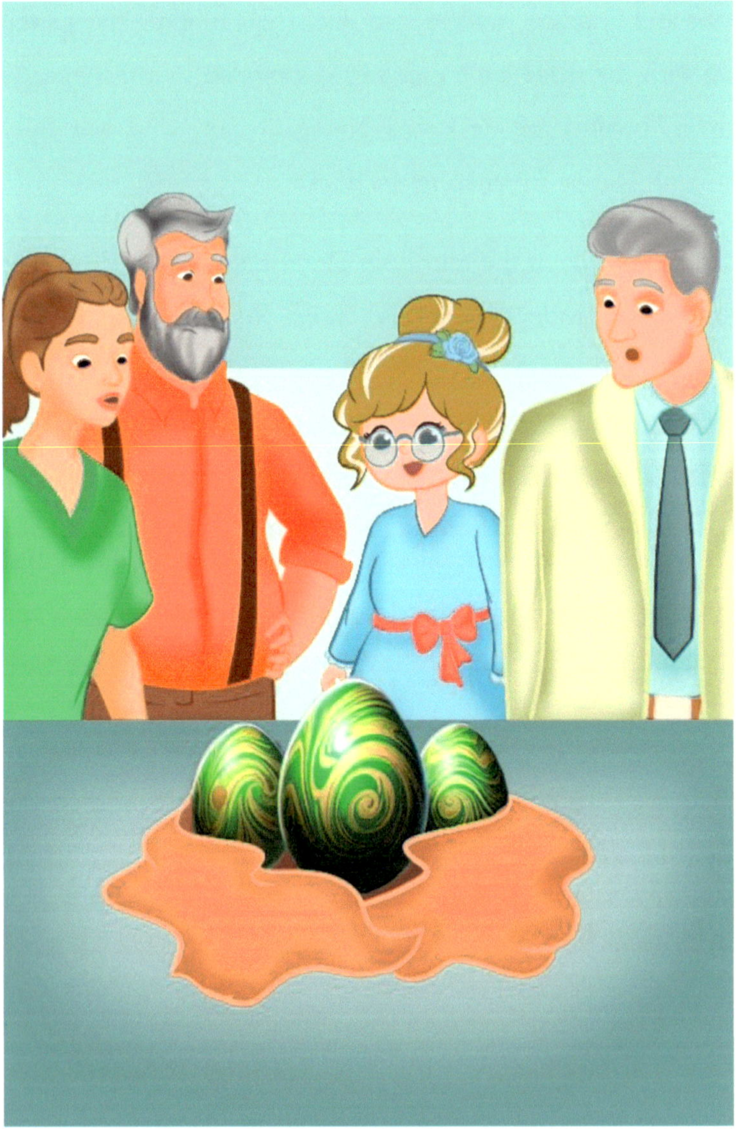

Doc Brian was surprised at what he saw. He looked at Pops, then Grammy, then back at the eggs, over and over, with both his mouth and eyes wide open, but no sound came out. Finally, Big Pops said to Doc Brian, "Well, I told you they were back, Doc."

Just then, Nurse Megan walked into the room to complain about Marley when she saw the three green eggs on the blanket on the table. With fear in her voice, Nurse Megan asked, "What are those green eggs?"

Nobody in the room was sure how to answer. Finally, Pops decided Nurse Megan needed to be told the truth. "Well, Megan, I'm going to tell you the truth. These green eggs are from a creature called The Hemple. The Hemple was believed to have disappeared many years ago. It's said that the Hemple was a magical creature, and no one alive today has ever seen a Hemple."

After hearing the story, Nurse Megan started jumping up and down excitedly, shouting about how she couldn't wait to tell everyone. After Pops calmed her down, Big Pops explained why everyone in that room must keep it a secret: *the eggs must stay hidden.*

The story passed down said the Hemple was a magical creature. It was green and not very big. It could fly like a bird, but it could also disappear and reappear anywhere. If you pet one, it would grant you one wish.

While everyone was talking at the same time about the eggs and the Hemple, Nurse Megan interrupted and asked, "Isn't this a good thing?"

Doc Brian answered, "Not if you're a mean and selfish person."

Grammy decided to tell the story her grammy used to tell her when she was a little girl. "There was a mean man named Lachinvar. Lachinvar took the Hemple for himself. He used its magic selfishly for his own riches, food, and many houses. He made all the rules so he had all the world's money and the biggest castles in all the lands.

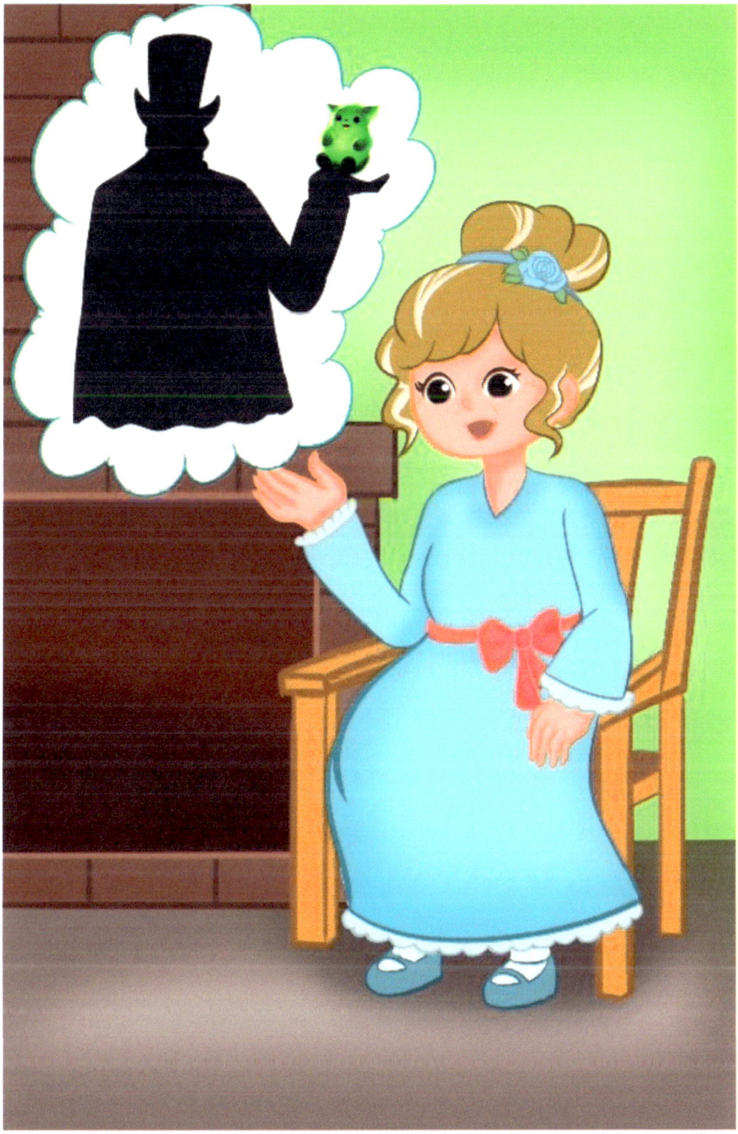

"Lachinvar seemed very happy but was missing one very important thing. He was missing love. No friends, no family, no love."

"One morning, Lachinvar woke up and rang the bell for his servant. He ordered the servant to bring him the Hemple at once. The Hemple's cage was brought and placed on the bed next to Lachinvar. With a big smile, he reached into the cage and rubbed the Hemple."

Then Lachinvar closed his eyes and wished for the prettiest, sweetest, most loving woman in the world to come to live with and love him. He opened his eyes, but there was nothing. Lachinvar tried again and again, day after day, but nothing happened. Growing angrier, he yelled for his smartest advisor and demanded to know why the Hemple wasn't granting his wish. The advisor explained that the only wish the Hemple couldn't grant was a wish for love.

The longer Lachinvar went without love, the sadder and lonelier he became. And the more lonely and sad he felt, the meaner he became. He started using the Hemple's magic to do very bad things. He bullied everyone around him. Eventually, all the people moved away, and Lachinvar was left completely alone and miserable. No one ever heard from Lachinvar again. Over time, people thought it was just a made-up fairy tale.

Until today.

Big Pops said, "We can never tell anyone about this because we don't want anyone stealing the eggs." Doc Brian carefully placed the green eggs in a special box to keep them warm until the baby Hemples were ready to be born. Nurse Megan asked, "When will the eggs hatch?" Everyone in the room exchanged glances, but no one really had an answer.

Doc Brian took out his special tool, the stethoscope, which lets him hear animals' hearts. He placed the end on each of the eggs and listened to all three Hemple eggs one by one. Finally, he scratched his chin and let out a deep sigh. "They're in there," he said, "but I have no idea when they might hatch. We'll just have to check every day."

Despite the excitement, Big Pops still seemed unhappy. Nurse Megan asked, "What's wrong, Big Pops?" After thinking for a moment, he said, "I'm afraid someone will find out."

Grammy and Doc Brian tried to reassure him that everything would be okay. But then Big Pops asked, "What happens when the eggs hatch and we have three baby Hemples?" Doc Brian smiled and whispered, "We'll have to wait and see."

Every day, Nurse Megan would open the office and go straight to the special box keeping the Hemple eggs warm. She hoped and prayed the eggs would hatch soon.

After six long months, the day finally arrived. When Nurse Megan opened the office and went to the special box, she saw that each Hemple egg had a large crack. Overjoyed, she couldn't wait for Doc Brian to arrive so he could use his stethoscope and listen to the eggs.

When Doc Brian walked through the front door, Nurse Megan excitedly grabbed his arm and dragged him into the office with the special box holding the Hemple eggs. "Look, look!" she shouted. "Cracks in all three eggs!" Jumping up and down, she begged him to hurry and listen to the eggs.

Just like before, Doc Brian listened to the first egg, then the second, and finally the third. This time, he stood up and asked Nurse Megan to close all the curtains, lock the doors, and cancel all the appointments. "Oh, and don't forget to put the 'Closed' sign on the front door," he added.

While Nurse Megan did that, Doc Brian called Big Pops and Grammy, telling them, "It's time."

When Grammy and Big Pops arrived, they saw even more cracks in each Hemple egg. Stroking his chin, Doc Brian observed that all three eggs seemed to be cracking in the same way at the same time. He was relieved, thinking that the only people who knew about the Hemple eggs were the ones in the room.

But that wasn't exactly true.

Outside, standing beneath the window, was Big Pops and Grammy's granddaughter, Abigail. Her parents, Nicole and Tim, had let her spend time with Pops, Grammy, Uncle Doc Brian, and Aunt Nurse Megan, who even let her help around the office. Today, Abigail decided to play a joke and surprise Uncle Brian and Aunt Megan. She had hidden in the backseat of Pops' car, and because Grammy and Pops were in such a hurry, they hadn't noticed her.

Now, Abigail was hiding beneath the office window, peeking inside. She saw the special box holding the three cracked Hemple eggs, and she saw everyone gathered around. Though she couldn't hear anything, she could see everything that was happening.

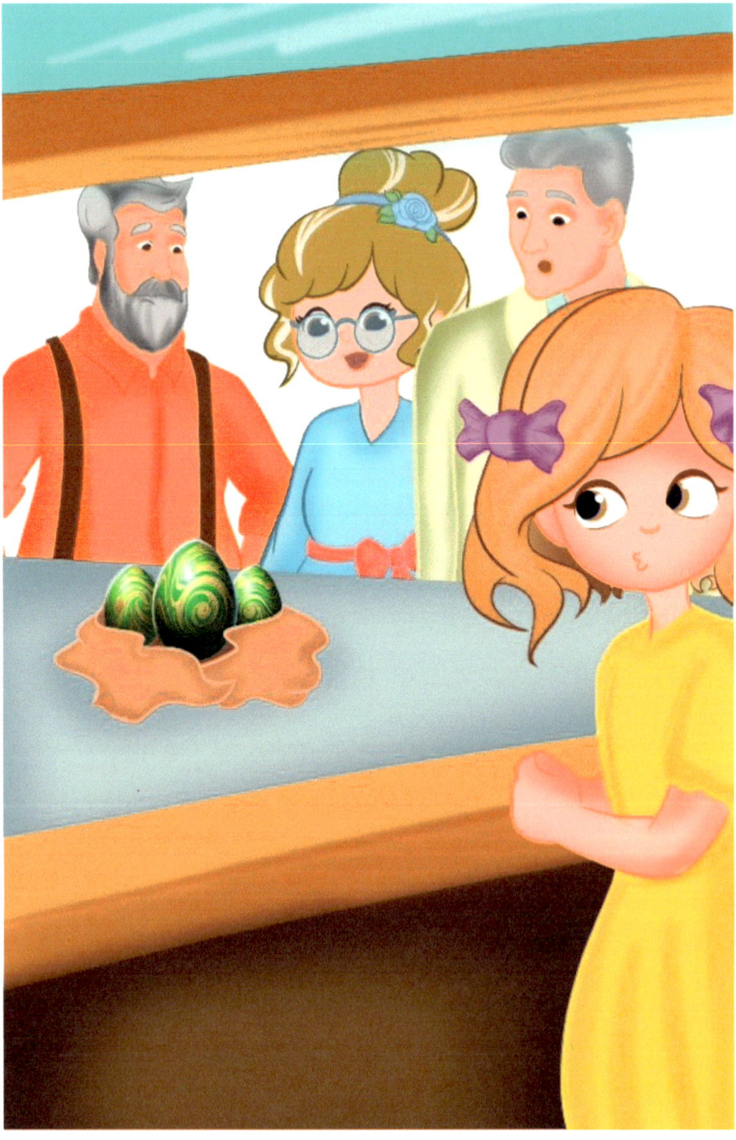

After about 30 minutes, Abigail peeked inside again, and what she saw was magical. Three Hemple eggs had fully hatched, revealing three small, green creatures that looked a bit like birds but not quite. To her, they looked like stuffed toys—but they were real.

Just as the last Hemple broke free from its shell, Big Pops glanced out the window at the same moment Abigail looked in. They locked eyes. Startled, Abigail ran away before Big Pops could stop her.

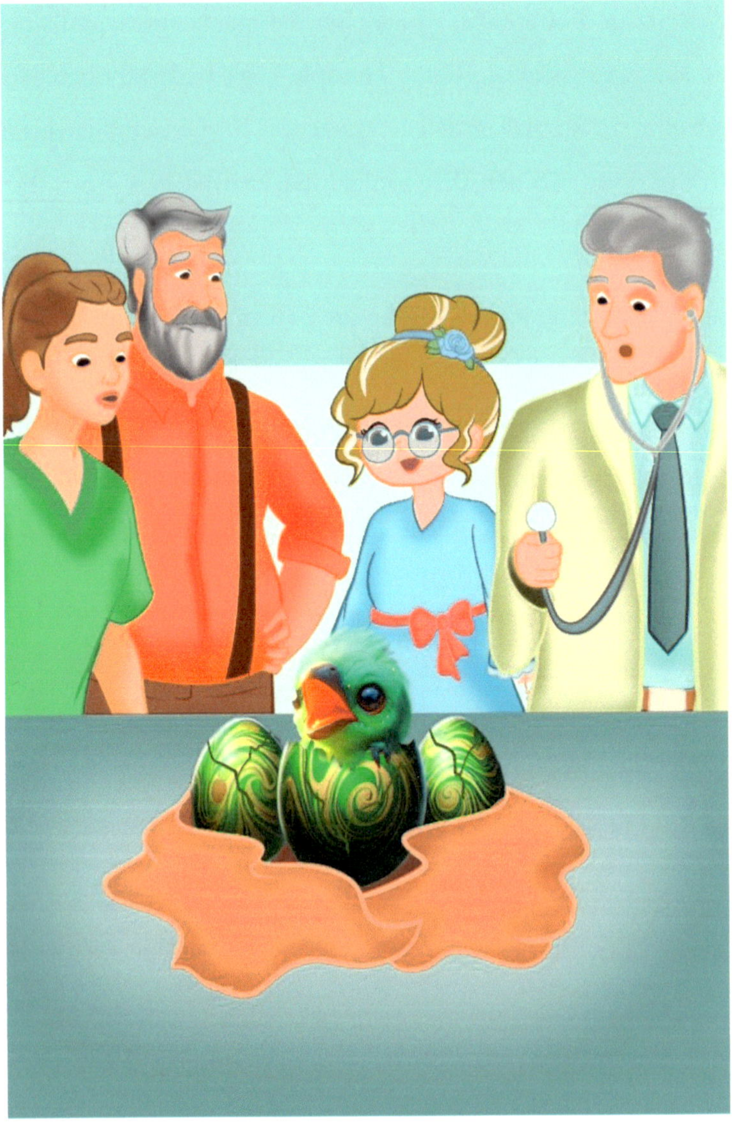

Big Pops never mentioned to anyone that he had seen Abigail.

Doc Brian, Big Pops, and Grammy put on gloves, and each picked up a Hemple. They all knew that a Hemple had to be fully grown to grant wishes. Without a mother, the baby Hemples needed very special care. Nurse Megan decided that if they worked together, four caregivers would be better than one.

Four days after the Hemples were born, Nurse Megan was serving breakfast to her niece Abigail, who was sleeping over. Abigail was quietly drawing at the table. Aunt Megan peeked over at the picture and asked Abigail what she was drawing. Abigail suddenly got very quiet and covered the picture. Aunt Megan tried harder to catch a glimpse, but Abigail crumpled up the drawing and started to leave the room.

Aunt Megan stopped her and insisted on seeing the picture. With tears in her eyes, Abigail reluctantly handed over the crumpled paper. Not knowing what it was, Aunt Megan felt nervous. As she uncrumpled the paper, she noticed Abigail was still crying, her tears flowing down her cheeks.

To Aunt Megan's shock, when she uncrumpled the paper, it was a picture of three green eggs, cracked open, with baby Hemples inside. Aunt Megan's eyes widened, and she asked, "Abby, sweetie, what are those three green fuzzy birds in your picture?"

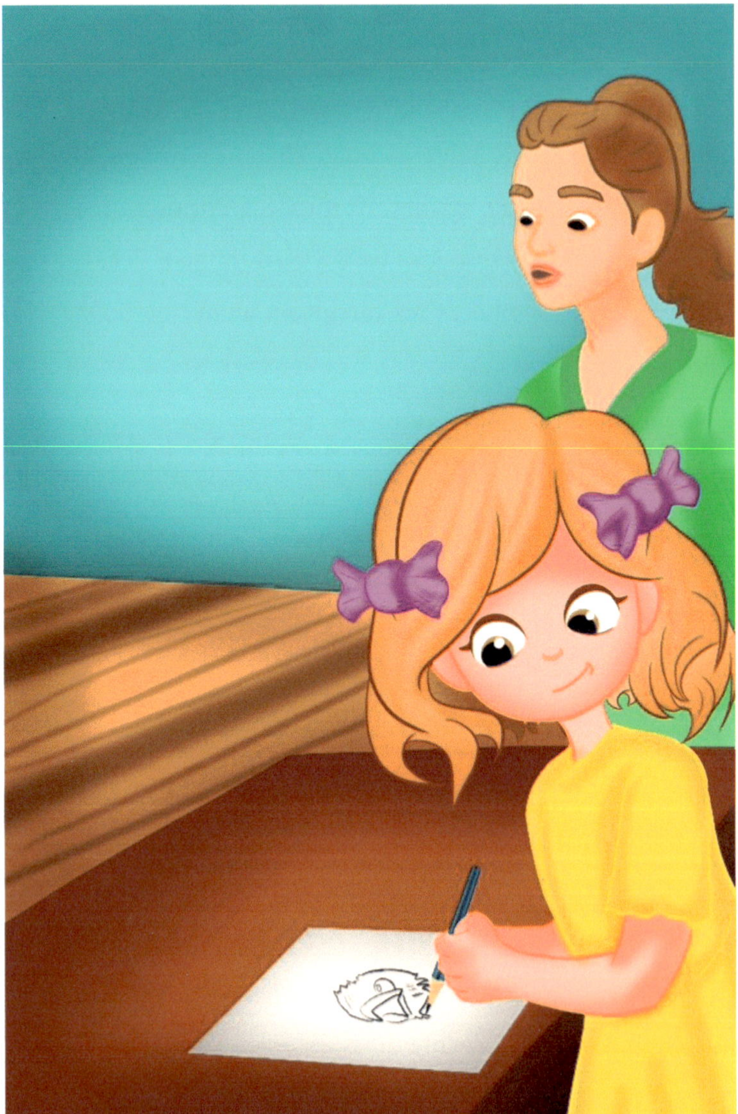

Abigail cried even harder. Aunt Megan gently said, "Abigail, honey, please stop crying and just tell Aunt Megan the truth." Finally, after some more comforting, Abigail admitted to being under the window at Uncle Brian's office the day the three green eggs hatched. She explained that she saw everything, and when Big Pops noticed her, she got scared and ran away, hoping Big Pops wouldn't be mad at her. The more Abigail talked, the more she cried.

Aunt Megan reassured her, saying, "You did nothing wrong, sweetheart, and Uncle Brian won't be mad."

However, Aunt Megan grew worried now that Abigail knew about the Hemples' birth. Megan thought she would go to work and tell Uncle Brian about it because he always knew what to do.

One urgent problem, though, was that Abigail was going to a birthday party for her friend Jane. There was a big chance Abigail might talk about the Hemples at the party. Aunt Megan decided to make Abigail promise to keep the green eggs a secret. She made her promise over and over, and Abigail agreed.

When Nurse Megan arrived at the office, she told Doc Brian what had happened. He didn't seem too worried but decided to call Big Pops just in case. Big Pops remembered seeing

Abigail that day but had forgotten to talk to her. He told Doc Brian not to worry, that he'd chat with his granddaughter later.

That evening, Aunt Megan had to work late, so Abigail's mommy, Nicole, her daddy, Tim, and her new baby brother, Jack, went to the park to pick Abigail up from the party. Later, Nicole called Megan and told her that when they arrived at the party, everyone was talking about three green fuzzy things that Abigail apparently couldn't stop mentioning. She kept talking about the three fuzzy creatures that came from three green eggs that had hatched.

Nicole and Tim thought Abby's imagination was just running wild, but the problem was that she wouldn't stop talking about it. She seemed so sure about the green eggs and how they hatched.

Megan's response shocked Abigail's parents: "She's not making it up."

After explaining the Hemples to Nicole and Tim, they were asked to come to Doc Brian's with Abigail. Nicole and Tim still thought it was a prank until they walked in and saw the warm box holding the three green Hemple eggs. Pops asked Abigail's parents to please just tell Abby they are special green birds, and that's it.

Tim then asked, "Well, um, is there more to it than green birds? Because that's already strange." Then Pops went on to explain to them the truth about the special wish powers.

Abigail was told she was mistaken about the wishes and that the Hemples were just special green birds. The next day, when Abigail went to school, all her friends teased her and said she made up the whole thing, which was great for keeping the secret but not so great for poor Abigail.

As the days and months passed, the three Hemples were growing, and as they grew, they looked less like birds and more like Hemples. At 10 months old, they grew to the size of a small dog, which is as big as they will get. Abigail got very attached to the Hemples and tried hard every day to see them if she could. She would feed them, care for them, and spend hours just talking to them. It was almost as though the Hemples understood.

Abigail decided it was time to name her new green friends. The names chosen were Willow, Piper, and Autumn. Doc Brian had a history book on Hemples that he gave to Abigail. The things she learned were so interesting. Abby learned the Hemples came from the D.D.A.J. Islands, named after a family of explorers who were siblings: David, Daniel, Avi, and Jiam Hemple.

One day, Abigail was feeding the one she called Autumn, but since they looked so much alike, it was very hard to know which was which. As she sat there petting Autumn, she wished she could tell the Hemples apart. Then, like magic, there was a puff of smoke, and each Hemple had a collar with their names, so now she could tell them apart. Just then, Grammy walked into the room and saw that each Hemple had their own bright, shiny collar with their very own names.

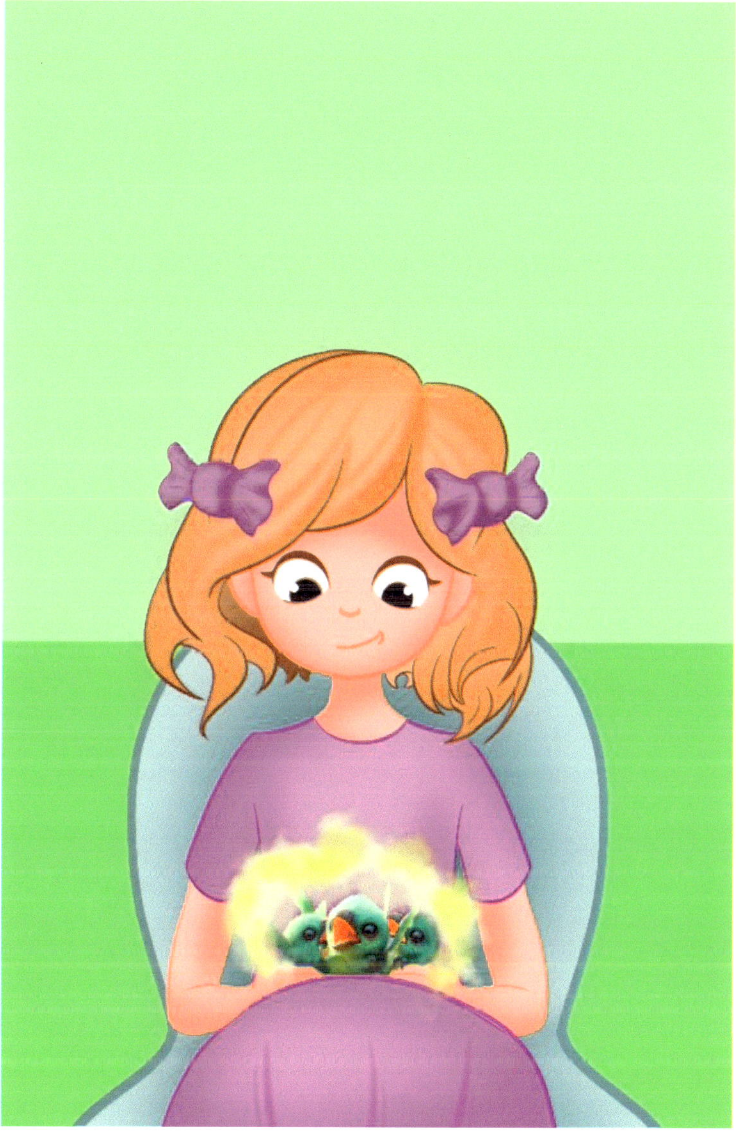

When Grammy asked Abigail where the collars came from, Abigail told Grammy, "I wished I could tell them apart, then there was a puff of smoke, and each Hemple had a new collar with their names."

Now, the Hemples were kind of flying around the office, getting in the way of everybody. Doc Brian and Big Pops decided the only safe thing to do was to drive the Hemples as far away as possible and let them live peacefully, far from any bad wish-makers. Abigail had one more day left to take care of Willow, Piper, and Autumn before they would be taken away. She took each one, placed them on her lap, and sang to them until she finally fell asleep.

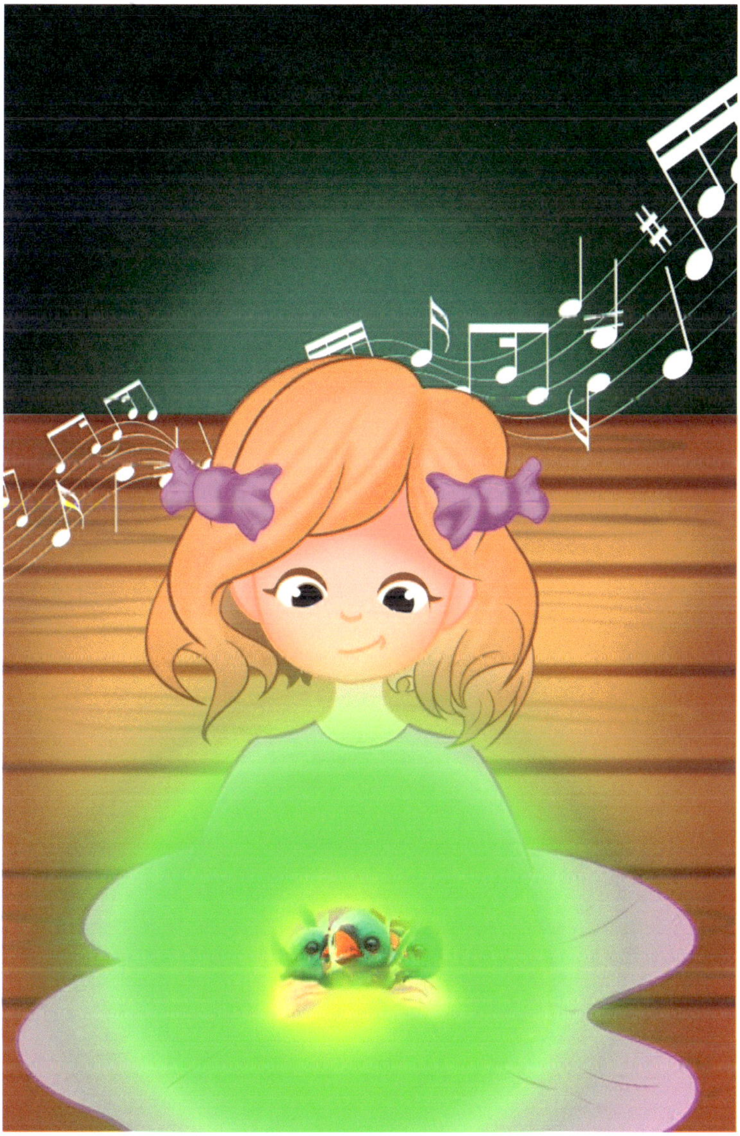

Doc Brian and Big Pops put the Hemples in the car. They drove and drove and just kept driving. They drove until they found the highest mountain, with the tallest trees and flowers and other trees everywhere.

There were so many green plants that nobody would ever notice the Hemples. Big Pops and Doc Brian decided to let the Hemples go but spent the night to make sure they were alright. In the morning, Doc Brian woke up first.

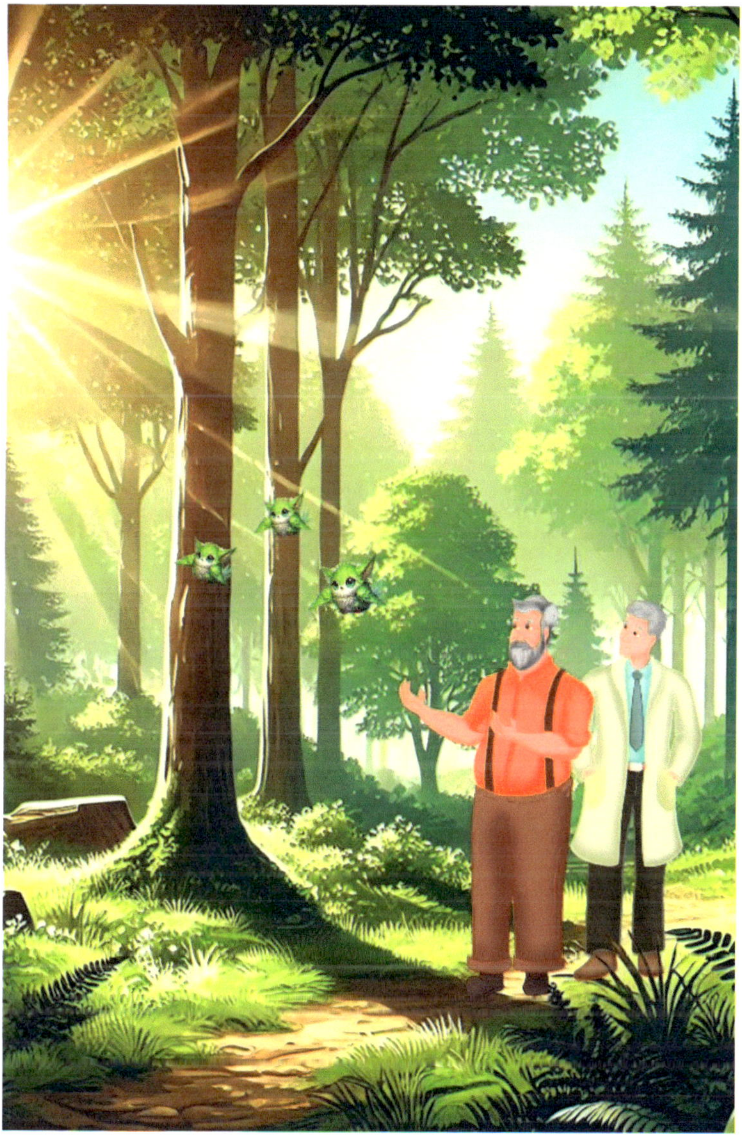

He went outside, looked around, and couldn't see any Hemples anywhere. Big Pops woke up, and Doc Brian explained that he had woken up early, gone outside, and the Hemples were gone, probably playing in the forest. The men walked around for a while but couldn't find them.

Back at the office, Doc Brian opened the door and noticed a light on in one of the exam rooms. As they got closer to the room, they heard strange noises and carefully opened the door to peek inside. They were shocked and surprised because sitting on the exam table were Piper, Willow, and Autumn, just staring at the two men who were staring back at them.

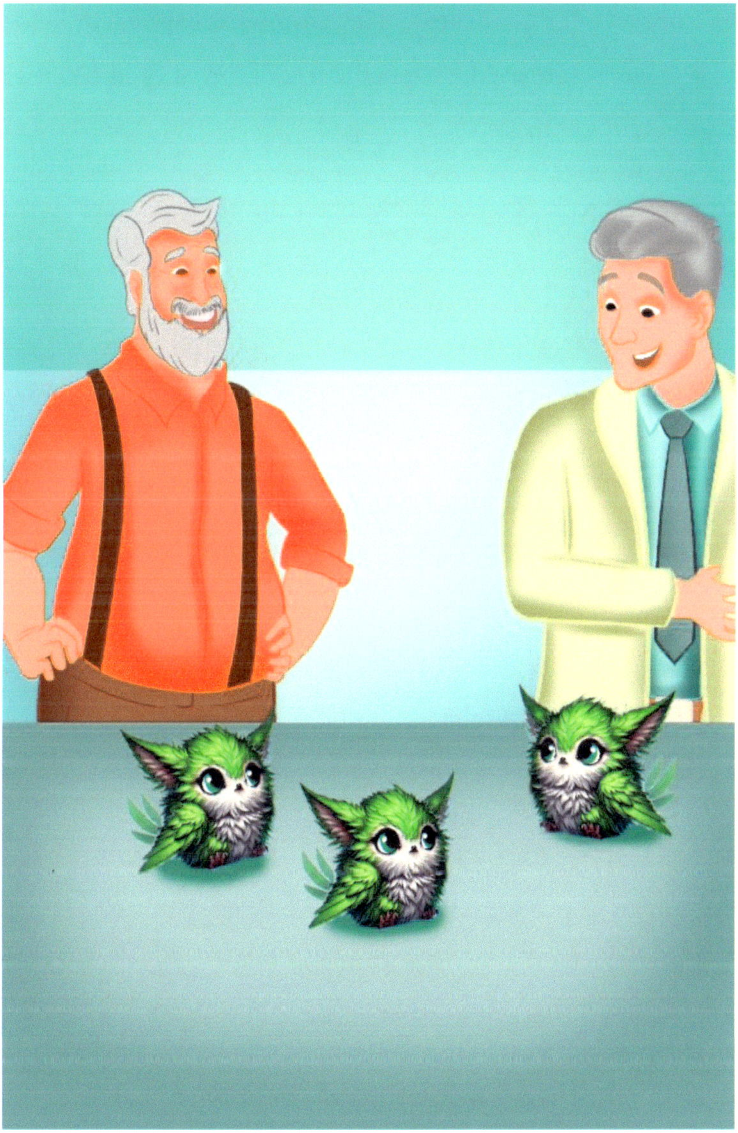

Big Pops let out a big bellow, "Hey Doc, what happened?" Doc Brian, just as surprised, snapped back, "How should I know? I'm a vet, not a magician!

Now, they were going to have to do this all over again tomorrow.

The very next morning, they did it all over again. After checking the car thoroughly, the boys came home confident that the Hemples were happily playing in the Great Forest. After the long ride home, they laughed about whether the Hemples might come back, which Doc Brian and Big Pops knew couldn't happen. Together, they walked into the same exam room where the light was on, only to find the Hemples sitting on the table, looking right back at them.

Doc Brian and Big Pops gathered everyone who knew the Hemples' secret to come to the office and discuss what to do. In the exam room were Big Pops, Doc Brian, Grammy, Nurse Megan, Abigail, Nicole, and Tim. Big Pops seemed the most worried about these magical Hemples.

Abigail, on the other hand, was so excited because the Hemples needed care, and she couldn't wait to help. Now, all the adults were worried, as there was no good plan except to keep the Hemples here in Data.

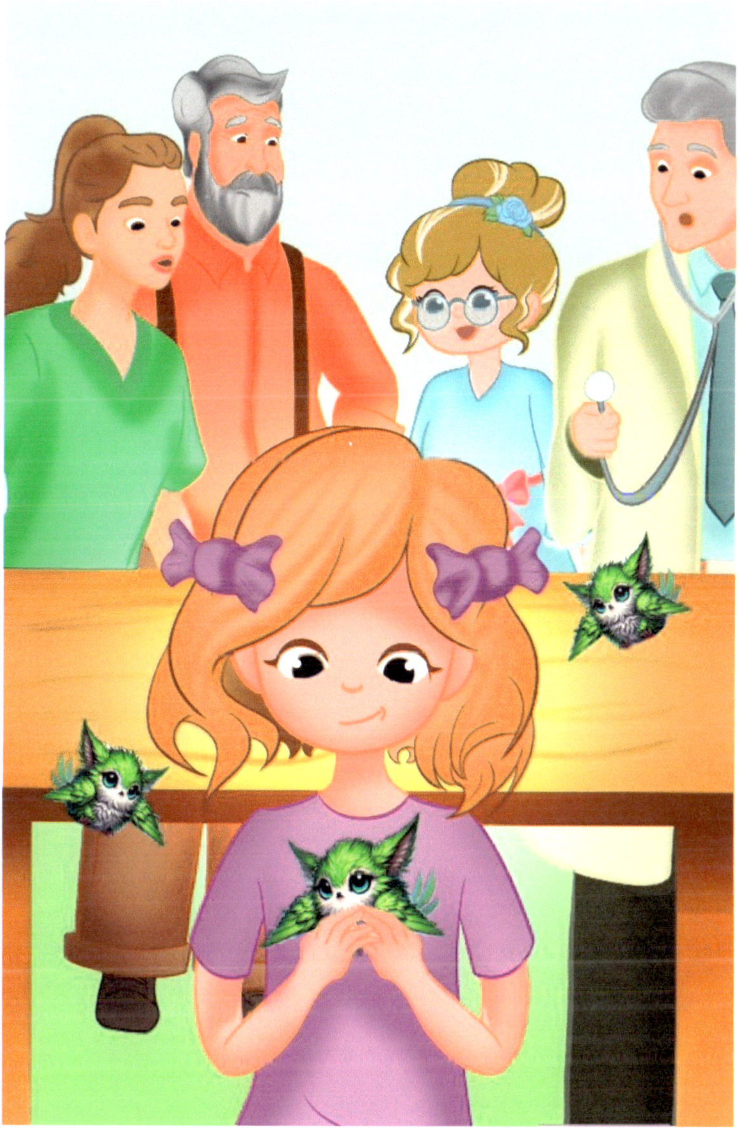

Abigail was so happy that she started singing a song: "A Hemple here, a Hemple there, oh, I love the Hemples and their green hair!"

She couldn't stop hugging Willow, Piper, and Autumn and wished the Hemples would never leave. The adults never realized that it was Abigail's wish to keep those cute green furry Hemples from leaving Data.

The End (for now).

Made in the USA
Columbia, SC
17 February 2025